Martyn Lewis

Virgin

First published in 1995 by
Virgin Books
an imprint of Virgin Publishing Ltd
332 Ladbroke Grove
London W10 5AH

A catalogue record for this book is available from the British Library.

ISBN 0 86369 943 X

Questions and answers edited by Tim Pollitt.

Designed by Design 23, London
Printed in England by Butler and Tanner, Frome, Somerset.

CONTENTS

INTRODUCTION

If you've picked up this book for a quick browse, the chances are you are one of the three million regular viewers of *Today's The Day*, the BBC nostalgia quiz that offers unrivalled trips down memory lane. Many of the programme's fans don't just tune in at 4pm every weekday – you write to us with your own memories, triggered by some event, person or programme unearthed by our researchers from the depths of the video vaults. For example, a clip of Britain's first quads prompted a splendid letter from one of them with the news that all were alive and well and now in their sixties; the family of a beauty queen from the fifties wrote about their delight at seeing for the first time "moving pictures" of granny in her younger days; and another family watching a report on the first boatload of bananas to arrive in Britain after the Second World War spotted their grandfather unloading one of the crates!

Other viewers write to tell us you'd like to take part as contestants, and – yes – we are gradually working our way through the formidable list! Clearly it is only a matter of time before some of you want MY job too!

Well – here's your chance!

This *Today's The Day* book offers an opportunity for someone in your family to take over as quiz master – to trigger some great memories without having Lewis in your living room! Famous Faces, the Video Wall, questions for every day of the year – all the ammunition you need to set up your very own *Today's The Day* is just a few pages away. And the book is laced with more than 150 photographs – old and not so old- specially researched by the programme's enthusiastic production team.

When *Today's The Day* first hit the TV screens more than two years ago, none of us predicted the scale of the hit afternoon show we would have on our hands. We couldn't do it without you – our loyal viewers. So this book is for you – let the memories flow!

Martyn Lewis

JANUARY

QUICK FIRE QUESTIONS

1 January
Which popular music show, presented by Jimmy Savile, went on the air for the first time today in 1964?

2 January
Which comedian, who died today in 1983, created the larger than life characters Old Lampwick, Mr Crump and Farmer Finks?

3 January
Born today in 1883, who succeeded Winston Churchill as Prime Minister immediately after World War II?

4 January
The television comedy *One Foot in the Grave* was first broadcast today in 1990. Name the actor who plays Victor Meldrew.

5 January
The death of Edward the Confessor on this day led to the Norman Conquests, but what was the year?

6 January
Jacques Delors became President of which government body today in 1985?

7 January
British naturalist Gerald Durrell was born today in 1925. What humorous memoir about his childhood in Corfu did he write?

8 January
Galileo died today in 1642. A spacecraft named after him was launched in 1989 on a journey to which planet?

9 January
Today in 1965 an experimental speed limit of 70mph was introduced on Britain's motorways. What is the speed limit on single carriage roads?

FAMOUS FACES

10 January

Ⓐ Today in 1955, it was announced that Muffin the Mule's new owner was likely to be Mollie Blake, the daughter of his creator. Who created him?

Ⓑ Sir Clive Sinclair launched his innovative C5 today in 1985. What was it?

Ⓒ On this day in 1993, out-going President George Bush announced that America's 'special relationship' with Britain would still exist under Bill Clinton. In which year was Bush voted President?

Ⓓ Today in 1963, Joan Plowright gave birth to a baby girl, Tamsin. In which film did Joan Plowright play the daughter of Archie Rice, a faded seaside comedian?

B

C

D

11 January
Born today in 1952, Ben Crenshaw is connected with which sport?

12 January
Today in 1935, who became the first woman to fly solo across the Pacific?

13 January
Born today in 1926, who created Paddington Bear?

14 January
Which new invention was demonstrated for Queen Victoria at Osborne House on the Isle of Wight today in 1878?

15 January
Greek ship owner Aristotle Onassis was born today in 1906. His granddaughter is the sole surviving heir to the multi-million dollar fortune he amassed during his lifetime. What is her name?

16 January
From which London railway station, opened today in 1854, would you begin a direct journey to Cardiff?

ON THE BOX

17 January

Ⓐ Breakfast television *(right)* began in Britain today in 1983. Who was the regular astrologer on BBC's *Breakfast Time*?

Ⓑ Today in 1987 it was announced that Jill Gascoigne was to take over as the star of *42nd Street* in the West End. Name the spin-off from the television series *The Gentle Touch,* in which she co-starred with Leslie Ash.

Ⓒ Today in 1984, the theme tune to the ITV drama *Auf Wiedersehen, Pet* was a chart hit. Name the song and the singer.

A

18 January

Prince Edward *(left)* moved into show business on this day in 1988. What was the name of the theatre company that he joined?

19 January

Who became Prime Minister of India on this day in 1966?

PICTURE WALL

20 January

Ⓐ Geoffrey Boycott looked forward to his testimonial year with Yorkshire today in 1984. What is the name of Yorkshire's cricket ground in Leeds?

Ⓑ Here is Roger Moore, with fellow cast-member Diana Morrison, between rehearsals for his West End debut in *Aspects of Love* today in 1989. Unfortunately, he was said to be unable to cope with 'the technical side of the singing' and didn't make it through to the opening night. Which song from the show went to number two in the charts that year?

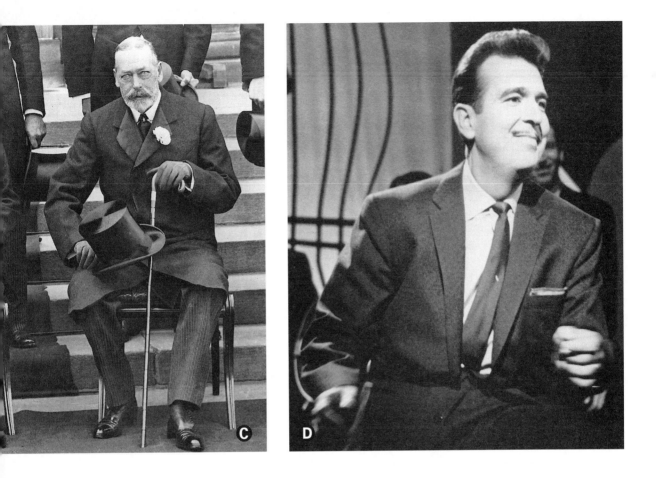

© King George V died at Sandringham on this day. What was the year?

Ⓓ Tennessee Ernie Ford took 'Sixteen Tons' to the top of the UK charts today in 1956. Can you name his first UK number one hit?

21 January
Comedian Vic Reeves was born on this day in 1959. What is the name of his comedy partner?

22 January
Ramsay MacDonald *(right)* took office today in 1924 as Britain's first Labour Prime Minister. Whom did he succeed?

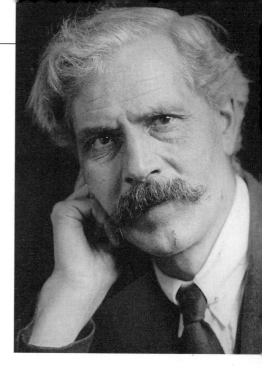

23 January
A painting by Edvard Munch, who died today in 1944, was stolen from Oslo's National Museum in February 1944 and recovered three months later. Name it.

BEAT THE CLOCK

24 January
Today in 1972 the treasures of which Egyptian king arrived in London for an exhibition?

25 January
Today in 1966, 21-year-old Tim Rice and 17-year-old Andrew Lloyd Webber *(right)* announced that they were to collaborate on which full-scale musical based on a biblical character?

26 January
English physician Dr Edward Jenner died today in 1823. What was the medical process that he pioneered?

27 January
Children's author Revd Charles Dodgson was born today in 1832. By what name is he better known?

28 January
The film *Carry On, Cleo* went on general release on this day in 1965. Which member of the Carry On team had the catchphrase, 'Stop messing about'?

29 January
Actor Tom Selleck was born today in 1945. Name the 1987 film in which he co-starred with Ted Danson and Steve Guttenberg.

30 January
Mount Etna erupted on this day in 1974. On which Mediterranean island is the volcano situated?

31 January
This photograph *(right)* shows the sculptures of the lions around the base of Nelson's Column in London when they first appeared today in 1867. Who designed them?

JANUARY ANSWERS

QUICK FIRE QUESTIONS

1 January
Top of the Pops.

2 January
Dick Emery.

3 January
Clement Attlee.

4 January
Richard Wilson.

5 January
1066.

6 January
The European Commission.

7 January
My Family and Other Animals.

8 January
Jupiter.

9 January
60mph.

FAMOUS FACES

10 January
(A) Annette Mills.
(B) An electric trike.
(C) 1988.
(D) *The Entertainer.*

● ●

11 January
Golf.

12 January
Amelia Earhart.

13 January
Michael Bond.

14 January
The telephone.

15 January
Athina Onassis Roussel.

16 January
Paddington.

ON THE BOX

17 January

Ⓐ Russell Grant.
Ⓑ *CATS Eyes*.
Ⓒ 'That's Living Alright',
   sung by Joe Fagin.

●●●●●●●●●●●●●●●●●●●●●

18 January
The Really Useful Theatre Company.

19 January
Mrs Indira Gandhi.

PICTURE WALL

20 January
Ⓐ Headingley.
Ⓑ 'Love Changes Everything',
   sung by Michael Ball.
Ⓒ 1936.
Ⓓ 'Give Me Your Word.'

●●●●●●●●●●●●●●●●●●●●●●●

21 January
Bob Mortimer.

22 January
Stanley Baldwin.

23 January
The Scream or *The Cry*.

BEAT THE CLOCK

24 January
Tutankhamen.

25 January
Joseph and the Amazing Technicolour Dreamcoat.

26 January
Vaccination.

27 January
Lewis Carroll.

28 January
Kenneth Williams.

29 January
Three Men and a Baby.

30 January
Sicily.

31 January
Sir Edwin Landseer.

FEBRUARY

1 February
In which country was Ronnie Biggs *(below)* arrested today in 1974?

2 February
Which South African President lifted the ban on the ANC on this day in 1990?

ON THE BOX

3 February

Ⓐ British actor Jeremy Kemp was born today in 1935. Can you name the character he played in BBC's *Z Cars*?

Ⓑ The popular drama series *Macmillan and Wife* was on TV today in 1976. Who played Macmillan?

Ⓒ Actor Gary Webster *(right)* was born today in 1964. In which series does he play Ray Daley?

● ●

4 February

Which flamboyant musician died on this day in 1987 and is associated with candelabras and piano-shaped swimming pools?

5 February

Name the American heiress kidnapped in San Francisco today in 1974 by an urban guerrilla group.

QUICK FIRE QUESTIONS

6 February

James II acceded to the throne on this day in 1685, but had to leave it hurriedly during the Glorious Revolution three years later. Can you name his father?

7 February

Which British author, born today in 1812, rose from humble beginnings to become the renowned author of over fifteen novels and numerous other works, including *Sketches by Boz*?

8 February

Entertainer Leslie Welch, famous for his exceptional recall and known as 'The Memory Man', died today in 1980. Which Hitchcock film features a character called Mr. Memory?

9 February

Which athlete, awarded the MBE today in 1982, won a gold medal for the 1500 metres at the Moscow Olympics?

10 February

It was announced on this day in 1965 that Millicent Martin was to part from her husband, Ronnie Carroll. On which 1960s TV programme did she first find fame singing the opening satirical song?

11 February

Margaret Thatcher became the first woman to lead a major British political party today in 1975. What was her maiden name?

12 February

American President Abraham Lincoln was born today in 1809. In which American city was he assassinated?

13 February

The infamous female Dutch spy, Margaretha Gertruida Zelle, was arrested on this day in 1917. By what name was she better known?

14 February

Michael Caine and the former James Bond, Sean Connery, were starring in the film *The Man who Would be King* on this day in 1976. Who wrote the original story?

15 February

The British explorer Ernest Shackleton was born today in 1874. In 1901 he was a member of a team who set off for the Antarctic in their attempt to reach the South Pole. Who commanded that expedition?

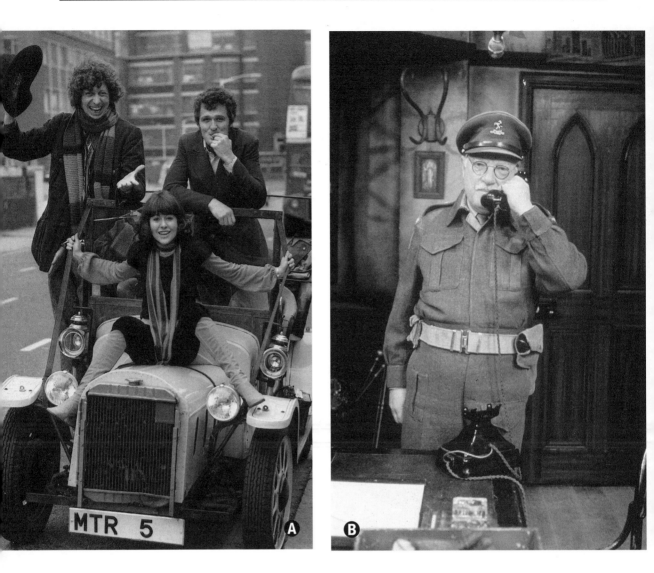

PICTURE WALL

16 February

Ⓐ It was announced today in 1974 that Tom Baker was to be the new Doctor Who. Whom did he succeed in that role?

Ⓑ A memorial service took place on this day in 1984 for the actor John le Mesurier. Which character did he play in the hit TV comedy series *Dad's Army*?

© Tennis player John McEnroe was born today in 1959. In which year did he win the Men's Singles Championship for the first of three times?

Ⓓ On this day in 1961, the film *Flaming Star* with Elvis Presley, was on general release. What was the title of Elvis's first film, which was released in 1956?

17 February

The artist Graham Sutherland died today in 1980. Where would you find his largest religious work, the tapestry *Christ in Glory*?

18 February

Which legendary Italian sports car manufacturer was born today in 1889?

19 February

The picture *(below)* shows the original cast of BBC's *EastEnders*, which was first broadcast today in 1985. Name the actress who plays Pauline Fowler, whose previous roles include Miss Brahms in *Are You Being Served*?

20 February

Today in 1947, Lord Mountbatten was appointed Viceroy of India. On the same day in 1960, his wife died. What was her first name?

FAMOUS FACES

21 February

Ⓐ Today in 1972, ex-Monkee Davy Jones rushed back to England from Hollywood to play his first straight part in London's West End. Ten years earlier, Jones had been in the first-ever episode of which popular TV police drama?

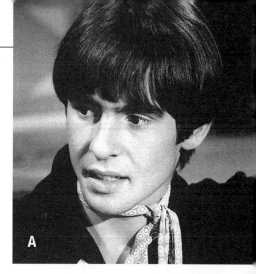

A

Ⓑ Actress Elizabeth Taylor married Michael Wilding today in 1952. How times has she been married to how many husbands?

Ⓒ British fighter pilot Douglas Bader, one of the heroes of the Battle of Britain, was born today in 1910. What is the name of his film biography?

Ⓓ The late actor *Mark McManus* was born on this day in 1935. What is the name of his most famous TV character?

B

C

D

BEAT THE CLOCK

22 February

The actress Drew Barrymore was born on this day in 1975. In which film did she co-star with an alien?

23 February

Which former US Defence Secretary was invested with an honorary knighthood today in 1988?

24 February

Prince Charles and Lady Diana Spencer *(below)* announced their engagement today in 1981. Name the Princess of Wales' step-grandmother.

25 February
Which British novelist, screenwriter, composer and critic, born today in 1917, achieved notoriety with *A Clockwork Orange*?

26 February
The Grand National was first held today in 1839. Name the only horse to have won the race three times.

27 February
Which organisation held its first session on this day in 1952 in its new head-quarters in New York?

28 February
Film director Vincente Minnelli *(right)* was born today in 1913. Who starred in his musical, *Meet Me in St Louis*, and later married him?

29 February
Italian composer Gioacchino Antonio Rossini, was born today in 1792. Who wrote the play upon which his opera *The Barber of Seville* was based?

FEBRUARY ANSWERS

1 February
Brazil.

2 February
President de Klerk.

ON THE BOX

3 February
Ⓐ PC Bob Steele.
Ⓑ Rock Hudson.
Ⓒ *Minder*.

●●●●●●●●●●●●●●●●●●●●●

4 February
Liberace.

5 February
Patty Hearst.

QUICK FIRE QUESTIONS

6 February
Charles I.

7 February
Charles Dickens.

8 February
The Thirty Nine Steps.

9 February
Sebastian Coe.

10 February
That Was the Week That Was.

11 February
Roberts.

12 February
Washington.

13 February
Mata Hari.

14 February
Rudyard Kipling.

15 February
Captain Robert Scott.

PICTURE WALL

16 February
Ⓐ Jon Pertwee.
Ⓑ Sergeant Wilson.
Ⓒ 1981.
Ⓓ *Love Me Tender.*

●●●●●●●●●●●●●●●●●●●●●

17 February
Coventry Cathedral.

18 February
Enzo Ferrari.

19 February
Wendy Richard.

20 February
Edwina.

FAMOUS FACES

21 February
Ⓐ *Z-Cars*.
Ⓑ Eight times to seven husbands.
Ⓒ *Reach for the Sky*.
Ⓓ (Detective Chief-Inspector) Jim Taggart.

BEAT THE CLOCK

22 February
E.T.

23 February
Casper Weinberger.

24 February
Barbara Cartland.

25 February
Anthony Burgess.

26 February
Red Rum – 1973; 1974; 1977

27 February
The United Nations.

28 February
Judy Garland.

29 February
Pierre-Augustin Caron de Beaumarchais

MARCH

1 March
Who was born today in 1904, became a famous bandleader and had 'Moonlight Serenade' as his signature tune?

2 March
Protesters were trying to prevent the motor company Land Rover being sold to an American company on this day in 1986. In which year, to the nearest five years, was the first Land Rover built?

3 March
Florida became the 27th US state today in 1845. It shares a border with two other states. One is Alabama but can you name the other one?

4 March
The Forth Railway Bridge was opened today in 1890. Which poet and designer, whose decorative prints are still produced, declared it 'the supremest specimen of all ugliness'?

5 March
Winston Churchill *(right)* today in 1946 declared an 'Iron Curtain had descended across Europe'. In which country was he speaking?

6 March
Name the author and singer who died today in 1967 and was famous for partnering Jeanette MacDonald in film operettas.

A

B

PICTURE WALL

7 March

Ⓐ England won their second successive Grand Slam rugby title today in 1992. Who was the last man before Will Carling to captain England to a Grand Slam?

Ⓑ The tennis player Ivan Lendl was born in Czechoslovakia on this day in 1960. How many times has he won the men's singles title at Wimbledon?

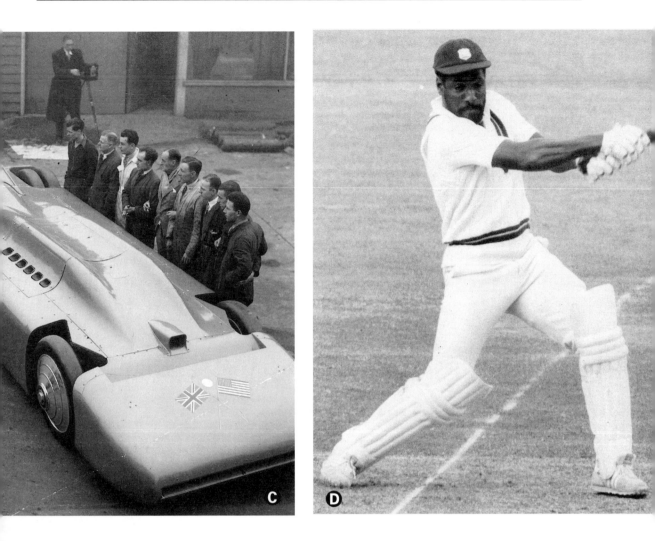

© Sir Malcolm Campbell attempted to break a land speed record today in 1935. What was the name of his vehicle?

Ⓓ The cricketer Viv Richards was born today in 1952. For which county did he play for twelve years?

BEAT THE CLOCK

8 March

Today in 1977, Princess Anne announced she was expecting her first child. The photograph *(below)* shows the royal family gathered for the christening. What was the baby called?

9 March

Russian cosmonaut Yuri Gagarin, *(right)* was born today in 1934. In which year did he become the first man in space?

10 March

The Prince of Wales, later King Edward VII, married the daughter of King Kristian IX of Denmark today in 1863. What was her name before her marriage?

11 March
Today in 1983, the newspapers reported that singer Bonnie Tyler was too weak to celebrate her UK number one hit as she was suffering from the flu. What was the title of the song? Was it 'Total Eclipse Of The Heart', 'It's A Heartache', or 'Lost In France'?

12 March
Paul McCartney married American photographer Linda Eastman today in 1969. To which red-haired actress had he once been engaged?

13 March
This actress and entertainer in the photograph, known as Two-Ton Tessie (right), was born today in 1914. What was her real name?

14 March
Javelin champion Tessa Sanderson was born today in 1956. She has competed in more Olympic Games than any other British athlete. How many times is that?

15 March
Novelist Dame Rebecca West died today in 1983. With which world-famous novelist did she have a celebrated affair?

ON THE BOX

16 March

Ⓐ Today in 1966, actor David McCallum received a Beatles-like welcome at London Airport *(above)* after living in Hollywood for three years. Which character in *The Man from UNCLE* was he playing at the time?

Ⓑ Leo McKern, who starred in the television drama series *Rumpole of the Bailey*, was born today in 1920. What was Rumpole's private name for his wife?

Ⓒ Jerry Lewis was born today in 1926. With whom did he team up to make a successful series of comedy films?

17 March

Clergyman Patrick Brontë was born today in 1777. Which of his three famous daughters wrote *Wuthering Heights*?

18 March

Today in 1930, American astronomer Clyde Tombaugh discovered a new planet, which is the outermost known in our solar system. What is it called?

19 March

Edgar Rice Burroughs, the novelist and creator of Tarzan, died today in 1950. Which French actor played the title role in the film *Greystoke: The Legend of Tarzan, Lord of the Apes*?

20 March

Today in 1945, Mandalay was recaptured by the British from the Japanese. It was once the capital of which country, now known as Myanmar?

21 March

Today in 1925 Murrayfield Stadium was officially opened. In which city would you find it?

FAMOUS FACES

22 March

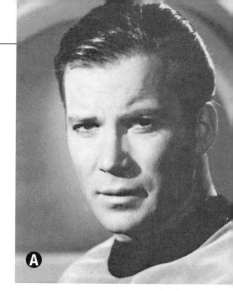

Ⓐ American actor William Shatner was born today in 1931. He is best known as Captain James T. Kirk in *Star Trek*, but he also starred in the title role of an American cop series in the 1980s. What was it called?

Ⓑ Today in 1983, Burt Reynolds was complaining in an interview that his beefcake image stopped people from taking him seriously. Six years earlier, he starred in a blockbuster chase comedy that went on to have two sequels. What was the name of the original film?

Ⓒ The American actor Karl Malden was born today in 1914. Name the television series in which he co-starred with Michael Douglas.

Ⓓ Today in 1987, Bob Hoskins won a Bafta Award for his role in which film produced by George Harrison's Handmade Films, that also starred Cathy Tyson and Michael Caine?

QUICK FIRE QUESTIONS

23 March
Today in 1961, plans were unveiled to make London's South Bank the 'greatest centre of culture in the world'. The Royal National Theatre has three theatres on the site: one is the Olivier, another the Cottesloe. Which is the third?

24 March
Queen Elizabeth I died at Richmond Palace today in 1603. Who succeeded her to the throne?

25 March
Born today in 1947, which singer-songwriter shared a number one hit with Kiki Dee in 1976 called 'Don't Go Breaking My Heart'?

26 March
In which city did Ludwig Van Beethoven die today in 1827?

27 March
English actor Michael York was born today in 1923. Can you name the American actress and singer with whom he co-starred in the musical film *Cabaret*?

28 March
Artist Marc Chagall died today in 1985. In which country was he born?

29 March
Architect Sir Edwin Lutyens was born today in 1869. Name the memorial in London's Whitehall that he designed.

30 March
Athlete Olga Korbut announced her retirement today in 1978. In which branch of sport did she win her Olympic gold medal?

31 March
The Eiffel Tower was inaugurated today in 1889. It was built to commemorate the French Revolution that began with the storming of which prison?

MARCH ANSWERS

1 March
Glenn Miller.

2 March
1947.

3 March
Georgia.

4 March
William Morris.

5 March
USA.

6 March
Nelson Eddy.

PICTURE WALL

7 March
Ⓐ Bill Beaumont.
Ⓑ None. It is the only major championship title that has eluded him.
Ⓒ *Bluebird*.
Ⓓ Somerset.

BEAT THE CLOCK

8 March
Peter.

9 March
1961.

10 March
Princess Alexandra of Denmark.

11 March
'Total Eclipse of the Heart'. It was her only UK number one.

12 March
Jane Asher.

13 March
Tessie O'Shea.

14 March
Five.

15 March
H. G. Wells.

ON THE BOX

16 March
Ⓐ Ilya Kuryakin.
Ⓑ She Who Must Be Obeyed.
Ⓒ Dean Martin.

●●●●●●●●●●●●●●●●●●●●●●●●

17 March
Emily.

18 March
Pluto.

19 March
Christopher Lambert.

20 March
Burma.

21 March
Edinburgh.

FAMOUS FACES

22 March
Ⓐ *T. J. Hooker.*
Ⓑ *Smokey and the Bandit.*
Ⓒ *The Streets of San Francisco.*
Ⓓ *Mona Lisa.*

QUICK FIRE QUESTIONS

23 March
The Lyttleton.

24 March
James I of England, who was also James VI of Scotland.

25 March
Elton John.

26 March
Vienna.

27 March
Liza Minnelli.

28 March
Russia.

29 March
The Cenotaph.

30 March
Gymnastics.

31 March
The Bastille.

APRIL

1 April

Name the actor, born in Bulgaria today in 1931, who became a household name playing Chief Inspector Wexford on television.

2 April

Actor Alec Guinness *(right)* was born today in 1914. Can you name the character he played in the television adaptation of John Le Carré's spy novel *Tinker, Tailor, Soldier, Spy*?

PICTURE WALL

3 April

Ⓐ Today in 1972, Charlie Chaplin returned to the United States after twenty years of self-imposed exile in which country?

Ⓑ Which German composer, who died today in 1950, collaborated with Bertolt Brecht to write *The Threepenny Opera* and *The Rise and Fall of the City of Mahagonny*?

Ⓒ Today in 1978, the Norwegian explorer Thor Heyerdahl burned his reed boat, *Tigris*, in protest at the war raging in the Horn of Africa. What is the name of the raft in which he made his famous trip from the Pacific Coast of South America to Polynesia?

Ⓓ Eddie Murphy was born today in 1961. In which 1982 film did he make his feature debut opposite Nick Nolte as a prisoner briefly released from jail on licence?

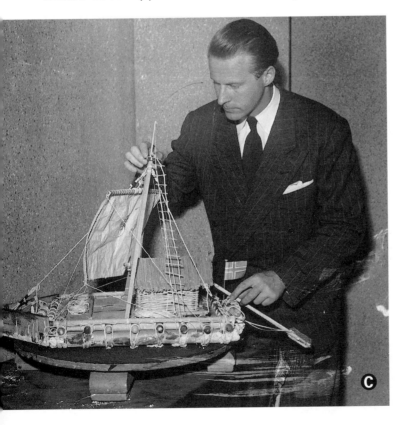

Ⓒ

Ⓓ

4 April

Today in 1957, the British government announced the end of National Service. In which year was it to be phased out?

5 April

Name the privately-owned West Sussex railway line which was given permission to link up with the British Rail network today in 1985.

6 April

The Church of Jesus Christ of Latter Day Saints was founded by Joseph Smith in Fayette, New York, today in 1830. By what name is this church more commonly known?

FAMOUS FACES

7 April

Ⓐ American film director Francis Ford Coppola was born today in 1939. Name the 1979 Vietnam war film which he described as being 'more of an experience than a movie'.

Ⓑ Today in 1963, it was announced that Connie Francis was to be sued for £17,000 by her promoters after she had given only twelve of her promised sixteen concerts on tour in South Africa. Which of her top ten hits was used as the title for a Dennis Potter drama serial?

© American singer Billie Holiday was born today in 1915. Name the film about her life, starring Diana Ross in the title role.

Ⓓ James 'Buster' Douglas was born today in 1960. Which undisputed World Heavyweight champion did he knock out?

QUICK FIRE QUESTIONS

8 April
Which American actor was elected Mayor of Carmel, California, today in 1986?

9 April
Born today in 1806, name the engineer of the Great Western Railway and designer of the Clifton Suspension Bridge.

10 April
Bananas were first displayed in a London shop window on this day, but what was the year?

11 April
Today in 1957, John Osborne's *The Entertainer* opened in London, starring which actor as Archie Rice, the music hall comedian?

12 April
Born today in 1941, which footballer captained England to victory against West Germany in the 1966 World Cup final?

13 April
Born today in 1917, which American actor and singer starred in *Showboat* and went on to play Clayton Farlow in *Dallas*?

14 April
Which British comic-strip hero, drawn by Frank Hampson, made his first appearance in the *Eagle* today in 1950?

15 April
Pop singer Marty Wilde was born today in 1939. His daughter Kim is also a singer. What was her first UK hit?

16 April
Today in 1969, who became the first Jamaican to reach the top of the UK singles charts with 'The Israelites'?

17 April
British actress Olivia Hussey was born today in 1951. She made her film debut seventeen years later in *Romeo and Juliet*. Who directed the film?

18 April
Which famous British bridge was sold to an American oil company today in 1968, and later re-erected in Arizona?

ON THE BOX

19 April
Ⓐ Hollywood actress Grace Kelly became a real-life princess today in 1956. What is the name of her husband?

Ⓑ Comedian Frankie Howerd *(right)* died today in 1992. What was the name of the 1970s television comedy series and film in which he played a wily slave in ancient Italy?

Ⓒ French chef Michel Roux was born today in 1941. What is the name of his equally famous brother?

BEAT THE CLOCK

20 April
American actor Ryan O'Neal was born today in 1941. In which 1971 film did he play opposite his ten-year-old daughter?

21 April
Television history was made today in 1964 when BBC launched its second channel. Which popular children's programme did it open with?

22 April
Today in 1969, which British yachtsman completed his non-stop solo round-the-world trip in Suhaili, after 312 days?

23 April
Born today in 1928, which child actress co-starred with Lionel Barrymore *(left)*, and grew up to become an American ambassador?

24 April
Name the pop song Paul McCartney *(left)* and Stevie Wonder took to the top of the UK charts today in 1982?

25 April
Anna Sewell died today in 1878. What is her most famous novel?

26 April
Born today in 1894, which Nazi leader was sentenced to life imprisonment at the Nuremberg Trials, and died in Spandau Prison in 1987?

27 April
Sheena Easton *(right)* was born today in 1959. She sang the theme for which James Bond film?

28 April
Who led the famous mutiny on HMS *Bounty* today in 1789?

29 April
Muhammad Ali was stripped of his World Heavyweight title today in 1967. Why?

30 April
Actor Leslie Grantham was born today in 1946. Which character did he play in the BBC soap *EastEnders*?

APRIL ANSWERS

1 April
George Baker.

2 April
George Smiley.

PICTURE WALL

3 April
Ⓐ Switzerland.
Ⓑ Kurt Weill.
Ⓒ *Kon-Tiki*.
Ⓓ *48 Hours*.

4 April
1962.

●●●●●●●●●●●●●●●●●●●●●●●●●●●●

5 April
The Bluebell Line.

6 April
The Mormon Church.

FAMOUS FACES

7 April
Ⓐ *Apocalypse Now*.
Ⓑ 'Lipstick On Your Collar.'
Ⓒ *Lady Sings the Blues*.
Ⓓ Mike Tyson.

QUICK FIRE QUESTIONS

8 April
Clint Eastwood.

9 April
Isambard Kingdom Brunel.

10 April
1633.

11 April
Laurence Oliver.

12 April
Bobby Moore.

13 April
Howard Keel.

14 April
Dan Dare.

15 April
'Kids In America.'

16 April
Desmond Dekker.

17 April
Franco Zeffirelli.

18 April
London Bridge.

ON THE BOX

19 April
Ⓐ Prince Rainier III of Monaco.
Ⓑ *Up Pompeii*.
Ⓒ Albert.

BEAT THE CLOCK

20 April
Paper Moon.

21 April
Play School.

22 April
Robin Knox-Johnston.

23 April
Shirley Temple Black.

24 April
'Ebony And Ivory.'

25 April
Black Beauty.

26 April
Rudolf Hess.

27 April
For Your Eyes Only.

28 April
Fletcher Christian.

29 April
He refused to be drafted into the US Army on religious grounds.

30 April
'Dirty' Den Watts.

MAY

1 May

Who was proclaimed Empress of India on this day in 1876?

2 May

What is the name of the American senator who died today in 1957 and was notorious for the Un-American Activities public hearings that he conducted in the early 1950s?

FAMOUS FACES

3 May

Ⓐ Born today in 1934, boxer Henry Cooper quit the ring after losing his British title to whom?

Ⓑ King George VI inaugurated the Festival of Britain in London today, which also marked the official opening of the Royal Festival Hall. Name the year.

© Richard D'Oyly Carte, the theatrical impresario, was born today in 1844. With whose operatic works is he associated?

Ⓓ Today in 1940, Flanagan and Allen were starring on the London stage. What was the comedy team they belonged to?

4 May
The Sears Tower was completed today in 1973. At the time it was the tallest building in the world. In which American city would you find it?

5 May
Alan Shepard *(right)* became the first American astronaut to travel in space in his mercury capsule on this day, but what was the year?

6 May
British actor James Stewart, better known as Stewart Granger, was born today in 1913. Which famous actress was he married to in the 1950s?

7 May
Today in 1969 Roger Miller entered the American country singles chart with his version of 'Me And Bobby McGee'. Who wrote the song?

8 May
Today in 1660 the British monarchy was restored after ten years of rule by Oliver Cromwell. Which king took the throne?

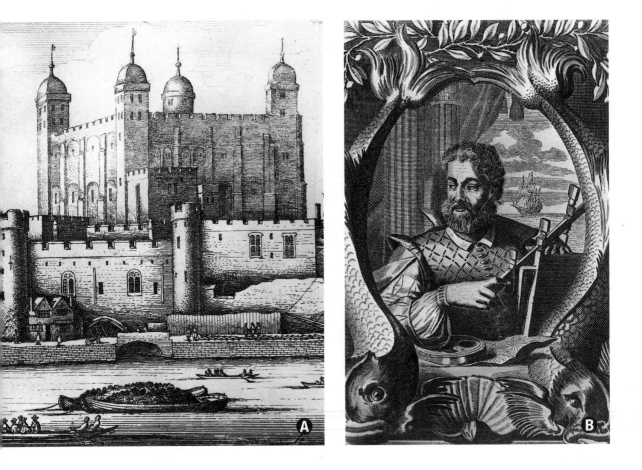

PICTURE WALL

9 May

Ⓐ Name the adventurer who stole the crown jewels from the Tower of London today in 1671.

Ⓑ Christopher Columbus began his fourth journey to the New World today in 1502. In which year did he set out for the Indies by sailing west?

© On this day impeachment proceedings began against President Nixon following the Watergate affair. Name the year.

Ⓓ Born today in 1873, which archaeologist discovered the tomb of Tutankhamen?

QUICK FIRE QUESTIONS

10 May
Today in 1970, Sir Noel Coward was honoured for outstanding services to British music at the Ivor Novello Awards. Which 1946 film, based on a play written by Coward, starred Celia Johnson and Trevor Howard?

11 May
The Highway Code was promoted for the first time by Herbert Morrison, the then Minister of Transport, on this day, but in which year?

12 May
English crime writer Leslie Charteris was born today in 1907. What is the name of his most famous fictional character known as the 'Saint'?

13 May
Name the British ex-pilot who was kidnapped in Beirut today in 1989.

14 May
Indecent Proposal was released today in 1993. Which actress, married to Bruce Willis, starred in it?

15 May
Edith Cresson became the first woman Prime Minister of France today in 1991. Whom did she succeed?

16 May
Tennis player Gabriella Sabatini was born today in 1970. What is her nationality?

17 May
Gary Cooper's funeral took place today in 1961. He won an Oscar for his role as a sheriff in which classic Western?

ON THE BOX

18 May

Ⓐ Today in 1990, Goldie Hawn had to slip out of a £5,000 dress when it got caught in a car door, and consequently attended the party in her underwear. On which American TV show did she first come to prominence?

Ⓑ Today in 1980, Sarah Greene (above) made her debut on *Blue Peter*. To which television presenter is she married?

Ⓒ Richard Chamberlain was starring on TV today in 1962 as which doctor?

19 May

Which Poet Laureate famous, for his love of architecture and old English churches, died today in 1984?

20 May

Singer and actress Cher was born today in 1946. Name her first husband with whom she sang in a successful pop duo.

21 May

Humphrey Bogart and Lauren Bacall *(below)* married today in 1945. On the set of which film did they meet and fall in love?

22 May

Born today in 1907, Laurence Olivier was awarded an honorary Oscar in 1946 for his outstanding achievement as the actor, director and producer of which film?

23 May

Which journalist and magazine proprietor, who died today in 1925, founded the *Picture Post*?

BEAT THE CLOCK

24 May
The funeral of which Indian leader took place today in 1991?

25 May
Today in 1988, which TV presenter was installed as the first female Rector of Edinburgh University?

26 May
Actor John Wayne *(above right)* was born today in 1907. What was his real name?

27 May
Born today in 1965, which Australian tennis player beat Ivan Lendl in the Men's Singles final at Wimbledon in 1987?

28 May
Comedian Eric Morecambe *(below right)* died today in 1984. What was his real name?

29 May
Sir Edmund Hillary and Sherpa Tenzing became the first climbers to reach the summit of Mount Everest on this day, but what was the year?

30 May
Henry VIII married Jane Seymour at Whitehall Palace today in 1536. What number wife was she?

31 May
Born today in 1922, actor Denholm Elliott starred in the film adaptation of *A Room with a View*. Who wrote the novel?

MAY ANSWERS

1 May
Queen Victoria.

2 May
Joseph McCarthy.

FAMOUS FACES

3 May
Ⓐ Joe Bugner.
Ⓑ 1951.
Ⓒ Gilbert and Sullivan.
Ⓓ The Crazy Gang.

●●●●●●●●●●●●●●●●●●●●●●●●●●

4 May
Chicago.

5 May
1961.

6 May
Jean Simmons.

7 May
Kris Kristofferson.

8 May
Charles II.

PICTURE WALL

9 May
Ⓐ Captain Blood.
Ⓑ 1492.
Ⓒ 1974.
Ⓓ Howard Carter.

QUICK FIRE QUESTIONS

10 May
Brief Encounter.

11 May
1931.

12 May
Simon Templar.

13 May
Jackie Mann.

14 May
Demi Moore.

15 May
Jacques Chirac.

16 May
Argentinian.

17 May
High Noon.

ON THE BOX

18 May
Ⓐ *Rowan and Martin's Laugh-in.*
Ⓑ Mike Smith.
Ⓒ Dr Kildare.

●●●●●●●●●●●●●●●●●●●●●

19 May
Sir John Betjeman.

20 May
Sonny Bono.

21 May
To Have and Have Not.

22 May
Henry V.

23 May
Edward Hulton.

BEAT THE CLOCK

24 May
Rajiv Gandhi.

25 May
Muriel Gray.

26 May
Marion Morrison.

27 May
Pat Cash.

28 May
Eric Bartholomew.

29 May
1953.

30 May
Number three.

31 May
E. M. Forster.

JUNE

ON THE BOX

1 June

Ⓐ Born today in 1944, who played Jesus of Nazareth in Franco Zeffirelli's film of the same name?

Ⓑ Today in 1992, Southfork Ranch was sold to an Arizonan businessman. It had provided the regular setting for which soap opera?

Ⓒ Today in 1976 it was announced that Sir Harold Wilson (left) would narrate a 13-part television series called A Prime Minister on Prime Ministers. Who succeeded him at Number 10?

●●●●●●●●●●●●●●●●●●●●●●●●●

QUICK FIRE QUESTIONS

2 June

Born today in 1941, who is the drummer of the Rolling Stones?

3 June

Born today in 1925, which American actor starred in the films The Boston Strangler and The Vikings?

4 June

Born today in 1738, which English king brought about the American War of Independence?

5 June
Who shot Robert Kennedy today in 1968?

6 June
Bjorn Borg was born today in 1956. How many times did he win the Men's Singles title at Wimbledon?

7 June
Born today in 1909, which actress won an Oscar for her role in *Driving Miss Daisy*?

8 June
Born today in 1869, name the American architect who designed the Guggenheim Museum in New York?

9 June
Hong Kong became a British colony today in 1898. In which year does China regain control of the colony?

10 June
Born today in 1922, which actress starred in *The Pirate* and *A Star is Born*?

11 June
Born today in 1910, which French undersea explorer won an Academy Award for his 1956 film *The Silent World*?

12 June
Which gangster was charged with 5,000 offences today in 1931?

13 June
Alexander the Great died today in 323BC. Of which great philosopher had he been a pupil?

14 June
Born today in 1811, Harriet Beecher Stowe wrote which famous anti-slavery novel?

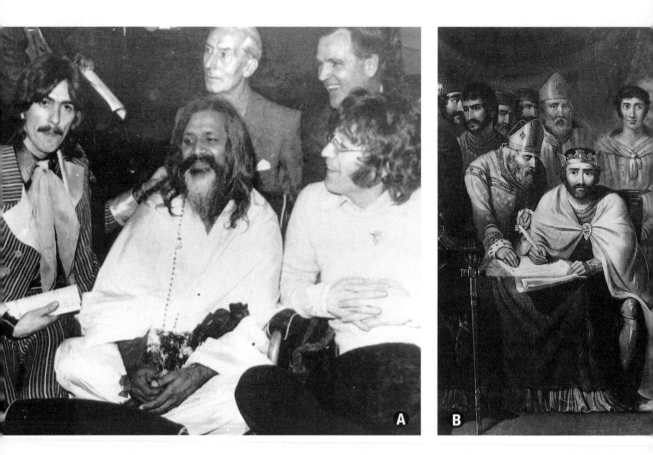

PICTURE WALL

15 June

Ⓐ Today in 1968, the Beatles finally renounced their association with the man who had become their spiritual guru. What was his name?

Ⓑ On this day the Magna Carta was signed by King John at Runnymede. In which year?

© Actor James Robertson Justice was born today in 1905. Name the irascible surgeon he played in the *Doctor* series of films.

Ⓓ Florence Nightingale opened her first school of nurses today in 1860. In 1907 she became the first woman to be given which honour?

16 June

The first Duke of Marlborough died today in 1722. Which of his descendants wrote the duke's biography over 200 years later?

17 June

Iceland became an independent republic today in 1944. Which state is its nearest European neighbour?

18 June

Today in 1815, the Duke of Wellington *(left)* finally defeated Napoleon at the Battle of Waterloo. To which South Atlantic island was Napoleon exiled?

19 June

Which pop group topped the UK singles charts today in 1971 with 'Chirpy Chirpy Cheep Cheep'?

20 June

This pilot *(below)* touched down at London Airport today in 1966, having become the first British woman to make a round-the-world solo flight. Name her.

FAMOUS FACES

21 June

Ⓐ George Michael lost his battle in the High Court with his record company, Sony, today in 1994. Name his singing partner in Wham!

Ⓑ Today in 1978, Elaine Page opened in the title role of *Evita*. Who played the part of Che Guevera?

A

B

Ⓒ French author Françoise Sagan was born today in 1935. What was the name of her first novel, which she published at the age of nineteen?

Ⓓ Prince William was born on this day in 1982. What is his position in line to the British throne?

BEAT THE CLOCK

22 June
Meryl Streep *(right)* was born today in 1949. Who starred opposite her in the 1979 tear-jerker *Kramer vs Kramer*, about the custody battle for a seven-year-old boy?

23 June
Today in 1960 Eddie Cochrane achieved posthumous success with a British number one. Name the song.

24 June
Today in 1955, the opera *Die Schweigsame Frau (The Silent Woman)* was premièred in Dresden. Who wrote it?

25 June
Dancer John Cranko died today in 1973. His first full length ballet was *Prince of the Pagodas* with music by which British composer?

26 June
Laurie Lee was born today in 1910. To which country, on the eve of civil war, did he travel in his autobiographical *As I Walked Out One Mid summer Morning*?

27 June
Which American President ordered the United States Air Force and Navy to Korea today in 1950?

28 June
Born today in 1909, which English novelist wrote *Epitaph for a Spy* and *The Intercom Conspiracy?*

29 June
Which female English poet wrote the poem 'Aurora Leigh' and died today in 1861?

30 June
Gone With the Wind was published today in 1936. What is the name of the heroine played by Vivien Leigh in the 1939 film?

JUNE ANSWERS

ON THE BOX

1 June
Ⓐ Robert Powell.
Ⓑ *Dallas*.
Ⓒ James Callaghan.

QUICK FIRE QUESTIONS

2 June
Charlie Watts.

3 June
Tony Curtis.

4 June
George III.

5 June
Sirhan Bishara Sirhan.

6 June
Five. 1976 – 1980.

7 June
Jessica Tandy.

8 June
Frank Lloyd Wright.

9 June
1997.

10 June
Judy Garland.

11 June
Jacques Cousteau.

12 June
Al Capone.

13 June
Aristotle.

14 June
Uncle Tom's Cabin.

PICTURE WALL

15 June
Ⓐ The Maharishi Mahesh Yogi.
Ⓑ 1215.
Ⓒ Sir Lancelot Spratt.
Ⓓ Order of Merit.

16 June
Winston Churchill.

17 June
The UK.

18 June
St. Helena.

19 June
Middle of the Road.

20 June
Sheila Scott.

FAMOUS FACES

21 June
Ⓐ Andrew Ridgeley.
Ⓑ David Essex.
Ⓒ *Bonjour Tristesse*.
Ⓓ He is second in line.

BEAT THE CLOCK

22 June
Dustin Hoffman.

23 June
'Three Steps To Heaven.'

24 June
Richard Strauss.

25 June
Benjamin Britten.

26 June
Spain.

27 June
President Harry S. Truman.

28 June
Eric Ambler.

29 June
Elizabeth Barrett Browning.

30 June
Scarlett O'Hara.

JULY

FAMOUS FACES

1 July

Ⓐ Actress Olivia de Havilland was born today in 1916. In a celebrated 1940s court case, she successfully sued which studio for refusing to release her at the end of a seven year contract?

Ⓑ Today in 1963, Kim Philby was named as the third man in the 'spy scandal' involving these two men. Who are they?

Ⓐ

Ⓑ

© On this day Virginia Wade won the Ladies' Singles title at the 100th Wimbledon Championships. In which year?

Ⓓ Actress Jean Marsh was born today in 1934. Which 1970s TV drama series did she create with Eileen Atkins?

BEAT THE CLOCK

2 July
Today in 1644 the Roundheads fought the Cavaliers at Marston Moor. Which side won?

3 July
Rolling Stone Brian Jones *(right)* died today in 1969. Who replaced him in the band?

4 July
Jazz musician Louis Armstrong *(below)* was born today in 1900. What was his nickname?

5 July

Designed by Renzo Piano and English architect Richard Rogers, which controversial arts centre is named after a French President who was born today in 1911?

6 July

The Russian pianist Vladimir Ashkenazy *(right)* was born today in 1937. What other strand did he add to his musical career in the 1970s?

7 July

The creator of Sherlock Holmes, Sir Arthur Conan Doyle, died today in 1930. Which actor, once married to actress Anna Massey, played the title role in Granada's successful television series *The Adventures of Sherlock Holmes*?

8 July

Name the author of *The Prisoner of Zenda*, who died today in 1933.

9 July

Former Prime Minister, Sir Edward Heath, was born today in 1916. Which religious publication did he edit from 1948 to 1949?

10 July

The German composer Carl Orff was born today in 1895. What is the name of his most famous work?

ON THE BOX

11 July

Ⓐ Andy Pandy *(above)* made his first television appearance today in 1950. What was the name of his rag doll friend?

Ⓑ Laurence Olivier died today in 1989. He won an Emmy in 1982 for his role in which TV drama series?

Ⓒ Name the television series in which John Stride, born today in 1936, played a tough, ambitious solicitor called David Main.

12 July
The film *When Harry Met Sally* was released today in 1989. The writer Nora Ephron also wrote a film based on the breakdown of her marriage to Watergate journalist Carl Bernstein. What is it called?

13 July
Ruth Ellis was the last woman to be executed today in Britain in 1955. Who played her in *Dance With a Stranger,* the film about her life?

14 July
Which sex symbol married the millionaire playboy Gunter Sachs today in 1966?

15 July
Lee Trevino won the British Open golf title today in 1972. In which year did he win it for the first time?

16 July
Ginger Rogers was born today in 1911. For which 1940 film did she receive her Academy Award?

17 July
Stirling Moss won his first Grand Prix today in 1955. Which Argentinian won the World Championship that year for the third of five times?

PICTURE WALL

18 July

Ⓐ The Spanish Civil War began today in 1936. Who led the rebellion against the republican government?

Ⓑ Adolf Hitler's *Mein Kampf* was published today in 1925. What career did Hitler pursue for the first few years of his adult life?

© Nelson Mandela was born today in 1918. He was elected President of South Africa in 1994. Whom did he succeed?

Ⓓ Today in 1971 was the last time that Pelé played football for Brazil. In which World Cup competition did he make his first appearance for that country?

QUICK FIRE QUESTIONS

19 July
What was the name of Henry VIII's flagship, which sank on this day in 1545 with the loss of over 700 lives?

20 July
Which *Kung Fu* film star was found dead in a Hong Kong apartment in 1973?

21 July
Sirimavo Bandaranaike became Prime Minister of Ceylon today in 1960. By what name is Ceylon now better known?

22 July
The American gangster John Dillinger was shot dead in Chicago in an ambush by FBI agents on this day in 1934. By what name was he generally known?

23 July
Which famous American novelist, born today in 1888, wrote *The Big Sleep*?

24 July
British actor Peter Sellers died today in 1980. In which 1963 film, directed by Stanley Kubrick, did he play three parts?

25 July
What was abolished in Tunisia today in 1957?

26 July
British author Aldous Huxley was born today in 1894. What is the title of his novel set in London's bohemia?

27 July
Which French-born novelist, poet and historian, who wrote *The Bad Child's Book of Verse*, died today in 1953?

28 July
Johann Sebastian Bach died today in 1750. How many children did he have?

29 July
Prince Charles married Lady Diana Spencer today in 1981. Who was their chief bridesmaid?

30 July
Emily Brontë was born today in 1818. In which Yorkshire village did her family live?

31 July
Which order of Catholic priests was founded by St Ignatius of Loyola, who died today in 1556?

JULY ANSWERS

FAMOUS FACES

1 July
Ⓐ Warner Bros.
Ⓑ Donald Maclean and Guy Burgess.
Ⓒ 1977.
Ⓓ *Upstairs, Downstairs*.

BEAT THE CLOCK

2 July
The Roundheads.

3 July
Mick Taylor.

4 July
Satchmo.

5 July
Georges Pompidou.

6 July
Conducting.

7 July
Jeremy Brett.

8 July
Anthony Hope.

9 July
The Church Times.

10 July
Carmina Burana.

ON THE BOX

11 July
Ⓐ Looby Loo.
Ⓑ *Brideshead Revisited*.
Ⓒ *The Main Chance*.

•••••••••••••••••••••••••

12 July
Heartburn.

13 July
Miranda Richardson.

14 July
Brigitte Bardot.

15 July
1971.

16 July
Kitty Foyle.

17 July
Juan Fangio.

PICTURE WALL

18 July
Ⓐ General Franco.
Ⓑ An artist.
Ⓒ Frederik Willem de Klerk.
Ⓓ Sweden 1958.

QUICK FIRE QUESTIONS

19 July
The Solent.

20 July
Bruce Lee.

21 July
Sri Lanka.

22 July
Public Enemy Number One.

23 July
Raymond Chandler.

24 July
Dr Strangelove.

25 July
The monarchy.

26 July
Antic Hay.

27 July
Hilaire Belloc.

28 July
20, but only 6 survived.

29 July
Lady Sarah Armstrong-Jones.

30 July
Howarth.

31 July
The Jesuits.

AUGUST

1 August

French designer Yves Saint Laurent was born today in 1936. Which Paris couturier employed him at the start of his career?

2 August

Born today in 1925, television globe-trotter Alan Whicker was a reporter on which BBC programme during the 1950s and '60s, before presenting his own show *Whicker's World*?

3 August

Today in 1914, the first ship passed through the Panama Canal. Name the two oceans which lie either side of the Canal.

4 August

John Lennon caused an outcry when he claimed today in 1966 that the Beatles were more popular than Jesus Christ. Who was his second wife?

FAMOUS FACES

5 August

Ⓐ Marilyn Monroe died today in 1962. She starred with Jack Lemmon and Tony Curtis in the film *Some Like it Hot*. Who directed it?

Ⓑ Born today in 1930, Neil Armstrong was the first man to set foot on the moon, but in which year?

Ⓒ Actress Joan Hickson was born today in 1906. What is the first name of her unassuming TV detective, Miss Marple?

Ⓓ Director John Huston (*above*) was born today in 1906. Who were the two stars of his 1985 film *Prizzi's Honour*?

● ●

6 August
Lord Alfred Tennyson was born today in 1809. To whose memory was his famous poem 'In Memoriam' dedicated?

7 August
Caroline of Brunswick (*left*) died today in 1821. To whom was she married?

8 August
Dustin Hoffman was born today in 1937. With whom did he star in *Midnight Cowboy*?

BEAT THE CLOCK

9 August

Today in 1957 American actress Tippi Hedren gave birth to a baby girl who grew up to become which famous actress?

10 August

Born today in 1911, in what professional capacity has Marjorie Proops *(below)* been offering advice to the nation for over 40 years?

11 August

Author Alex Haley was born today in 1921. What is the name of the young slave to whom he traced his origins in his epic novel *Roots*?

12 August

Novelist Ian Fleming, most famous for creating James Bond, died today in 1964. What was the title of the first Bond novel to be made into a film?

13 August

Dr Fidel Castro was born today in 1927. He is President of which country?

14 August

The picture *(below)* shows Lord Northcliffe, who died today in 1922. In what industry did he achieve distinction?

15 August

T. E. Lawrence, the soldier and writer, was born today in 1888. Who played him in David Lean's film *Lawrence of Arabia*?

16 August

Pete Best, the Beatles' original drummer, was sacked today in 1962. Who replaced him?

17 August

Harry Corbett, creator of puppets Sooty and Sweep *(below)*, died today in 1989. Who succeeded him as their guardian?

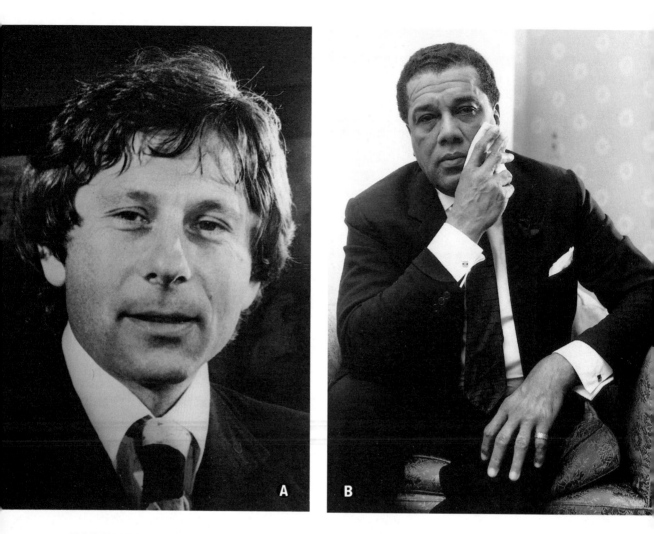

PICTURE WALL

18 August

Ⓐ Film director Roman Polanski was born today in 1933. Name his 1974 film starring Jack Nicholson and Faye Dunaway.

Ⓑ Pianist Leslie Hutchinson died today in 1969. By what nickname was he popularly known?

© Mongol Emperor Gengis Khan died today in 1227. Who played him in *Gengis Khan*, the1964 film about his life?

Ⓓ Which American town bought the liner Queen Mary today in 1967?

19 August

The musical *Camelot* opened in London today in 1964. Who played King Arthur in the film based on the show?

20 August

Which British conservationist, whose wife wrote the famous book *Born Free* about their life together in Kenya, died today in 1989?

ON THE BOX

21 August

Ⓐ Which British actress co-starred with David Naughton *(right)* in the film *An American Werewolf in London*, which was released today in 1981?

Ⓑ Born today in 1933, who presents the long-running BBC film series?

Ⓒ Today in 1971 Diana Ross took 'I'm Still Waiting' to the top of the UK charts. Name the 1978 remake of *The Wizard of Oz* in which she starred.

QUICK FIRE QUESTIONS

22 August
The infamous French prison Devil's Island released its last inmate today in 1953. Which film starred Dustin Hoffman and Steve McQueen as inmates?

23 August
Italian-born film star, whose real name was Rodolpho Alphonso Gughielmi di Valentia d'Antonguolla, died today in 1926, provoking mass despair among his millions of female fans. By which name did they know him?

24 August
Vesuvius erupted today in AD79, burying which cities under tons of volcanic ash?

25 August
Born today in 1930, who once said, 'I have always hated that damn James Bond'?

26 August
The first Baron Tweedsmuir, Governor-General of Canada, was born today in 1875. He was also the author of *Greenmantle* and *The Thirty Nine Steps*. By what name is he better known?

27 August
Born today in 1910, which grocer's daughter received the Nobel Peace Prize in 1979?

28 August
Today in 1952, a former pupil of Harrow School became king of which country?

29 August
British naturalist Sir Peter Scott, who died today in 1989, was the founder of which Wildfowl Trust?

30 August
Name the Woolworths heiress who divorced Cary Grant today in 1945.

31 August
Which Yorkshire-born sculptor died today in 1986?

AUGUST ANSWERS

1 August
Christian Dior.

2 August
BBC's *Tonight*.

3 August
The Pacific and the Atlantic Oceans.

4 August
Yoko Ono.

FAMOUS FACES

5 August
Ⓐ Billy Wilder.
Ⓑ 1969.
Ⓒ Jane.
Ⓓ Jack Nicholson and
   Kathleen Turner.

●●●●●●●●●●●●●●●●●●●●●●●●●

6 August
Arthur Hallam.

7 August
George IV.

8 August
Jon Voight.

BEAT THE CLOCK

9 August
Melanie Griffith.

10 August
As an agony aunt.

11 August
Kunta-Kinte.

12 August
Doctor No.

13 August
Cuba.

14 August
Newspaper publishing.

15 August
Peter O'Toole.

16 August
Ringo Starr.

17 August
His son, Matthew Corbett.

PICTURE WALL

18 August
Ⓐ *Chinatown.*
Ⓑ 'Hutch'.
Ⓒ Omar Sharif.
Ⓓ Long Beach, California.

•••••••••••••••••••••••

19 August
Richard Harris.

20 August
George Adamson.

ON THE BOX

21 August
Ⓐ Jenny Agutter.
Ⓑ Barry Norman.
Ⓒ *The Wiz.*

QUICK FIRE QUESTIONS

22 August
Papillon.

23 August
Rudolph Valentino.

24 August
Pompeii and Herculaneum.

25 August
Sean Connery.

26 August
John Buchan.

27 August
Mother Teresa.

28 August
King Hussein of Jordan.

29 August
Slimbridge, Gloucestershire.

30 August
Barbara Hutton.

31 August
Henry Moore.

SEPTEMBER

QUICK FIRE QUESTIONS

1 September
Louis XIV died today in 1715. By which other name is he often known?

2 September
The Great Fire of London began in a baker's shop in Pudding Lane today, but what was the year?

3 September
Who became the Salvation Army's first woman general today in 1935?

4 September
Kenneth Kendall became the first newsreader to appear on screen today in 1955. What adventure-based game show did he present with Anneka Rice?

5 September
American film director Paul Bern died today in 1932. Which famous actress did he marry in July of the same year?

6 September
The first cricket test match was played today in 1880 at The Oval, between which two sides?

7 September
Today in 1838, Grace Darling became the heroine of which lighthouse near Farne Island?

8 September
Today in 1960, publishers Penguin were charged with public obscenity over which book?

9 September
Today in 1975, Martina Navratilova defected to the West. In which Eastern European city was she born?

10 September
Today in 1972, Emerson Fittipaldi became the youngest every Formula One motor racing world champion. What is his nationality?

11 September
Which Scottish poet, born today in 1700, wrote the words to 'Rule Britannia'?

FAMOUS FACES

12 September
Ⓐ Maurice Chevalier was born today in 1888. He starred in the film *Gigi*. Who wrote the novel on which it was based?

Ⓑ Senator John Kennedy married Jacqueline Bouvier today in 1953 and became President of the United States in 1961. What was his middle name?

Ⓒ Name the actor who played Hopalong Cassidy on television and in films who died today in 1972.

Ⓓ American actor Anthony Perkins died today in 1992. Which character did he play in the *Psycho* films?

D

13 September
Born today in 1916, name the British author of children's books and 'unexpected tales' for adults.

14 September
The Hon. Angus Ogilvy was born today in 1928. To which member of the royal family is he married?

15 September
Agatha Christie *(right)* was born today in 1890. In what year did her play *The Mousetrap* begin its record-breaking run?

ON THE BOX

16 September

Ⓐ Born today in 1947, name the comedian who had a hit television comedy series which he called his *Mad House*?

Ⓑ Name this American actor *(below)*, born today in 1927, who made his name playing a detective in a dirty raincoat.

Ⓒ Born today in 1924, which American actress had a Broadway smash in the hit show *Applause*?

17 September

Today in 1961, one of the biggest ever ban-the-bomb demonstrations took place in London. Among those arrested was the ecclesiastical chairman of CND. Name him.

18 September

In which city was Greta Garbo born today in 1905?

19 September

Today in 1945, at the age of seventeen, Shirley Temple married which American film actor?

20 September

Kenneth More was born today in 1914. What was the name of the film in which he and three friends entered the London to Brighton vintage car race?

Ⓐ Ⓑ

PICTURE WALL

21 September

Ⓐ Bamber Gascoigne presented the first edition of *University Challenge* today in 1962. Who took over as the show's host in 1994?

Ⓑ Shirley Conran was born today in 1932. In which best-selling book, published in the 1970s, did she say, 'Life is too short to stuff a mushroom'?

© Today in 1915, for how much was Stonehenge sold at auction?

Ⓓ Larry Hagman was born today in 1931. Who was his famous mother?

BEAT THE CLOCK

22 September
The James Bond film, *Goldfinger*, was given its world première today in

1964. Sean Connery *(above)* played Bond. Which character did Honor Blackman *(left)* play?

23 September
The popular television quiz show, *Take Your Pick*, invited its contestants to 'open the box' for the first time today in 1955. Who was the presenter?

24 September
Which pop group took 'He Ain't Heavy, He's My Brother' to the top of the UK charts today in 1988?

25 September

Comedian Ronnie Barker was born today in 1929. Name the television comedy series in which he starred as a prison inmate *(left)* called Fletcher?

26 September

Children's author Hugh Lofting died today in 1947. He is best known for creating which fictional character?

27 September

Today in 1980 Denis Healey *(right)* was defeated by Tony Benn in the contest for deputy leader of the Labour Party. Who was Labour's leader at the time?

28 September

The French writer Prosper Mérimée was born today in 1803. Which of his works was adapted for an opera by Bizet?

29 September

Born today in 1935, which rock'n'roll singer and pianist is known as 'the Killer'?

30 September

Actress Rula Lenska was born today in 1947. She starred in a 1970s TV drama series about three female rock singers determined to make it to the top. What was it called?

SEPTEMBER ANSWERS

QUICK FIRE QUESTIONS

1 September
The Sun King.

2 September
1666.

3 September
Evangeline Booth.

4 September
Treasure Hunt.

5 September
Jean Harlow.

6 September
England and Australia.

7 September
Longstone Lighthouse.

8 September
Lady Chatterley's Lover by D.H. Lawrence.

9 September
Prague.

10 September
Brazilian.

11 September
James Thomson.

FAMOUS FACES

12 September
Ⓐ Sidonie Colette.
Ⓑ Fitzgerald.
Ⓒ William Boyd.
Ⓓ Norman Bates.

•••••••••••••••••••••••••••

13 September
Roald Dahl.

14 September
Princess Alexandra.

15 September
1952.

ON THE BOX

16 September
Ⓐ Russ Abbott.
Ⓑ Peter Falk.
Ⓒ Lauren Bacall.

17 September
Canon Collins.

18 September
Stockholm.

19 September
John Agar.

20 September
Genevieve.

●●●●●●●●●●●●●●●●●●●●●●

PICTURE WALL

21 September
Ⓐ Jeremy Paxman.
Ⓑ *Superwoman*.
Ⓒ £6,000.
Ⓓ Mary Martin.

BEAT THE CLOCK

22 September
Pussy Galore.

23 September
Michael Miles.

24 September
The Hollies.

25 September
Porridge.

26 September
Dr Dolittle.

27 September
Michael Foot.

28 September
Carmen.

29 September
Jerry Lee Lewis.

30 September
Rock Follies.

OCTOBER

1 October
Today in 1969. Concorde did what for the first time?

FAMOUS FACES

2 October
Ⓐ The rock singer Sting was born today in 1951. Name the drummer in his former pop group The Police.

Ⓑ Groucho Marx was born today in 1890. What was the Marx Brothers' first film?

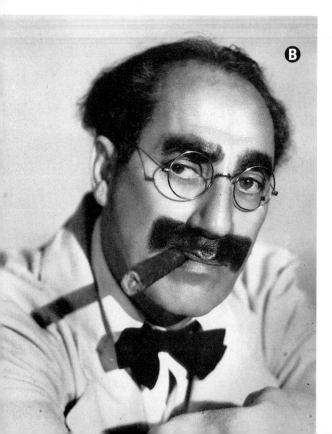

© The comic strip Peanuts was first published today in 1950. The picture shows the artist who created it. Name him.

Ⓒ

Ⓓ Today in 1836 the man pictured here returned from his five-year survey of the seas of South America in HMS *Beagle*. Who is he?

QUICK FIRE QUESTIONS

3 October
Vet and author James Herriot was born today in 1916. Who played Siegfried Farnon in the TV drama series *All Creatures Great and Small*, adapted from his books?

4 October
Buster Keaton was born today in 1895. Which famous comedian gave Keaton his start in films?

5 October
The first episode of *Monty Python's Flying Circus* was screened on television today in 1969. In which film did the comedy team recreate the New Testament?

6 October
Which nationalist, described as the 'uncrowned King of Ireland', died on this day in 1891?

7 October
Born today in 1931, which archbishop was awarded the Nobel Peace Prize in 1984?

8 October
London's Post Office Tower was the tallest building in Britain when it opened today in 1965. What is the tallest office building now?

9 October
HRH The Duke of Kent was born today in 1935. How is he related to the Queen?

10 October
Who wrote, produced, directed and starred in the film *Citizen Kane*, and died today in 1985?

11 October
Which French poet and playwright who wrote the screenplays of several films, including *Les Enfants Terribles*, died today in 1963?

ON THE BOX

12 October

Ⓐ Born today in 1929, which quizmaster is known for his catchphrase 'I've started so I'll finish'?

Ⓑ Operatic tenor Luciano Pavarotti *(below)*, born today in 1935, has performed several times as one of the Three Tenors. Can you name the other two?

Ⓒ Born today in 1944, Angela Rippon originally made her name as a newsreader, but on which famous Christmas show did she reveal that she was also a talented dancer?

13 October

Roman Emperor Claudius died today in AD54. Who played him in the classic BBC drama based on the book by Robert Graves?

14 October

Actress Dame Edith Evans died today in 1976. The picture *(right)* shows her in her most famous role as which character in Oscar Wilde's play *The Importance of Being Earnest*?

15 October

American composer Cole Porter died today in 1964. The song 'You're The Top' features in which of his shows?

16 October

Marie Antoinette was excecuted today in 1793. When told that her people had no bread, what is she alleged to have said?

17 October

Composer Frédéric Chopin died today in 1849. With which French novelist did he have a notorious relationship?

18 October

BBC TV detective series *Bergerac* was first shown today in 1981. Who played the title role?

19 October

Born today in 1931, who wrote *The Looking-Glass War* and *The Little Drummer Girl*?

PICTURE WALL

20 October

Ⓐ American singer Tom Petty was born today in 1953. What is the name of his backing band who have been with him for more than fifteen years?

Ⓑ Today in 1973, the Queen opened Sydney Opera House. In which Australian state is Sydney?

© Born today in 1822, who was the author of *Tom Brown's Schooldays*?

Ⓓ Entertainer Bud Flanagan, pictured here with his comic partner Chesney Allen, died today in 1968. His last recording was 'Who Do You Think You Are Kidding Mister Hitler' – the theme for which classic television comedy?

21 October
Alfred Nobel, the Swedish founder of the Nobel Prizes, was born today in 1833. Which Polish trade unionist was awarded a Nobel Peace Prize in 1983?

22 October
Born today in 1917, which British-born actress was the star of *Rebecca, Frenchman's Creek* and *Suspicion*?

BEAT THE CLOCK

23 October
The great cricketer W.G. Grace was born today in 1894. What do his initials stand for?

24 October
Actor Jack Warner *(right)* was born today in 1894. Can you name his famous actress sisters?

25 October
Born today in 1881, which Spanish artist, ceramicist and designer was one of the creators of Cubism?

26 October
The Beatles received their MBEs today in 1965 *(right)*. Which song was their first ever chart entry?

27 October
John Cleese was born today in 1939. In which film did he co-star with Jamie Lee Curtis, Kevin Kline and a goldfish?

28 October
Television presenter David Dimbleby was born today in 1938. His brother Jonathan is also well known on television. Here they are as children *(above)*. Who was their famous broadcaster father?

29 October
Actress and dancer Fanny Brice was born today in 1891. What is the name of the film made about her life, starring Barbra Streisand and Omar Sharif?

30 October
Today in 1938, Orson Welles broadcast which H.G. Wells story on the radio, causing mass panic in America?

31 October
The famous escapologist, Erich Weiss, died today in 1926. By what name is he better known?

OCTOBER ANSWERS

1 October
It broke the sound barrier.

FAMOUS FACES

2 October
Ⓐ Stewart Copeland.
Ⓑ *Coconuts*.
Ⓒ Charles Schultz.
Ⓓ Charles Darwin.

QUICK FIRE QUESTIONS

3 October
Robert Hardy.

4 October
Fatty Arbuckle.

5 October
Monty Python's Life of Brian.

6 October
Charles Stewart Parnell.

7 October
Archbishop of Cape Town, Reverend Desmond Tutu.

8 October
Canary Wharf.

9 October
First cousin.

10 October
Orson Welles.

11 October
Jean Cocteau.

ON THE BOX

12 October
Ⓐ Magnus Magnusson.
Ⓑ José Carreras and Placido Domingo.
Ⓒ *The Morecombe and Wise Christmas Show*.

• •

13 October
Derek Jacobi.

14 October
Lady Bracknell.

15 October
Anything Goes.

16 October
'Let them eat cake.'

17 October
George Sand.

18 October
John Nettles.

19 October
John Le Carré.

PICTURE WALL

20 October
Ⓐ The Heartbreakers.
Ⓑ New South Wales.
Ⓒ Thomas Hughes.
Ⓓ *Dad's Army.*

●●●●●●●●●●●●●●●●●●●●●●●●

21 October
Lech Walesa.

22 October
Joan Fontaine.

BEAT THE CLOCK

23 October
William Gilbert.

24 October
Elsie and Doris Waters.

25 October
Pablo Picasso.

26 October
'Love Me Do.'

27 October
A Fish Called Wanda.

28 October
Richard Dimbleby.

29 October
Funny Girl.

30 October
The War of the Worlds.

31 October
Harry Houdini.

NOVEMBER

PICTURE WALL

1 November

Ⓐ On this day, Sir Geoffrey Howe resigned from Margaret Thatcher's government. What was the year?

Ⓑ Phil Silvers died today in 1985. He was best known for his role as Sergeant Bilko. What was Bilko's first name?

© Golfer Gary Player was born today in 1935. What is his nationality?

© The gossip column writer Nigel Dempster was born today in 1941. In which newspaper does he write his column – the *Daily Mail* or the *Daily Express*?

2 November
Which Irishman, who died today in 1950, wrote *Pygmalion*?

3 November
Today in 1976, two French agents pleaded guilty to sinking the *Rainbow Warrior*, which was the flagship of Greenpeace. In which country did this act of sabotage take place?

4 November
General Charles de Gaulle *(left)* announced he was standing for re-election as President of France on this day, but what was the year?

5 November
Which former world chess champion beat Boris Spassky *(left)* in Belgrade today in 1922?

6 November
Born today in 1931, who directed the Oscar-winning film *The Graduate*?

FAMOUS FACES

7 November

Ⓐ Actor Steve McQueen died today in 1980. In which film did he play a prisoner of war who attempted to escape on a motorbike?

Ⓑ The singer and songwriter Joni Mitchell was born on this day in 1943. What is her nationality?

© The former model Jean Shrimpton was born today in 1942. She made her name in the 1960s, but what was her nickname?

Ⓓ Actress Su Pollard was born today in 1949. She played the part of Peggy in Hi-De-Hi! What was Peggy's ambition?

8 November
In Calcutta today in 1987, Australia won the Cricket World Cup for the first time. Who did they beat?

BEAT THE CLOCK

9 November
A group of suffragettes were caught throwing stones at the Guildhall in London during the Lord Mayor's banquet. What were they campaigning for?

10 November
The picture *(below)* shows journalist Henry Stanley finally tracking down the missing missionary Dr David Livingstone in Africa today in 1871. With which words did he greet him?

11 November
Which Soviet statesman said today in 1991, 'My life's work has been accomplished. I did all that I could'?

12 November
Which famous acrobat first performed his flying trapeze act in Paris today in 1859 and gave his name to a common item of athletic clothing?

13 November
Born today in 1850, who wrote *Treasure Island*?

14 November
The world's largest airport, King Khalid International Airport, was opened today in 1983 in Saudi Arabia's capital. What is the city called?

15 November
Leon Trotsky *(below)*, one of the original leaders of the Russian Revolution, was expelled from which political party today in 1927?

16 November
Today in 1988, the Queen was awarded £100,000 damages by which newspaper for printing one of her private photographs?

ON THE BOX

17 November

Ⓐ Today in 1975, advance bookings to see the film *Jaws* were breaking all records. What species of shark was Jaws?

Ⓑ Today in 1967, Disney's film *The Jungle Book* was showing in the cinemas. Who wrote the book on which the film was based?

Ⓒ Film director Martin Scorsese was born today in 1942. In his film *The Color of Money,* who starred as Fast Eddie Felson?

QUICK FIRE QUESTIONS

18 November
Car designer Sir Alec Issigonis was born today in 1906. In 1948, he designed the first British car to sell over a million models. Name the model?

19 November
Born today in 1962, which American actress won an Oscar for her role in *The Silence of the Lambs*?

20 November
Today in 1947 Princess Elizabeth married Lieutenant Philip Mountbatten. Who designed her wedding dress?

21 November
Born today in 1888, which Marx brother was renowned for never speaking in their films?

22 November
Which actor, who died today in 1976, was famous for playing Inspector Maigret in the 1960s TV series?

23 November
Which notorious American gunfighter was born William Bonney today in 1859?

24 November
Scott Joplin, the American ragtime pianist and composer, was born today in 1868. What was the name of his composition which was used as the title music to the film *The Sting*?

25 November
General Pinochet was born today in 1915. For sixteen years, he headed the military government of which country?

26 November
American bandleader Tommy Dorsey died today in 1956. With which instrument was he most associated?

27 November
Today in 1991, a fifteenth-century copy of which best-seller was sold in London for £1.1 million?

28 November
Enid Blyton, the prolific author of children's books, died today in 1968. What was the name of the policeman in her *Noddy* books?

29 November
Born today in 1895, which American director was famous for his choreography of dancing girls in film extravaganzas?

30 November
Who was born in Blenheim Palace today in 1874?

NOVEMBER ANSWERS

PICTURE WALL

1 November
Ⓐ 1990.
Ⓑ Ernie.
Ⓒ South African.
Ⓓ The *Daily Mail*.

••••••••••••••••••••••••••

2 November
George Bernard Shaw.

3 November
New Zealand.

4 November
1965.

5 November
Bobby Fischer.

6 November
Mike Nichols.

FAMOUS FACES

7 November
Ⓐ *The Great Escape*
Ⓑ Canadian.
Ⓒ The Shrimp.
Ⓓ To be made a Yellow Coat.

••••••••••••••••••••••••••

8 November
England (by seven runs).

BEAT THE CLOCK

9 November
Votes for women.

10 November
'Dr Livingstone, I presume.'

11 November
Mikhail Gorbachev.

12 November
Jules Léotard.

13 November
Robert Louis Stevenson.

14 November
Riyadh.

15 November
The Communist Party.

16 November
The *Sun*.

ON THE BOX

17 November
Ⓐ Great white shark.
Ⓑ Rudyard Kipling.
Ⓒ Paul Newman.

QUICK FIRE QUESTIONS

18 November
The Morris Minor.

19 November
Jodie Foster.

20 November
Norman Hartnell.

21 November
Harpo.

22 November
Rupert Davies.

23 November
Billy the Kid.

24 November
'The Entertainer.'

25 November
Chile.

26 November
The trombone.

27 November
The Bible.

28 November
P.C. Plod.

29 November
Busby Berkeley.

30 November
Sir Winston Churchill.

DECEMBER

QUICK FIRE QUESTIONS

1 December
Woody Allen was born today in 1935. Name his 1975 film which won three Oscars?

2 December
Today in 1965, which musical opened in London, starring Mary Martin and based on Thornton Wilder's play *The Matchmaker*?

3 December
Born today in 1857, which Polish-born author wrote *Lord Jim* and *Heart of Darkness*?

4 December
Born today in 1949, which American actor starred in *The Fabulous Baker Boys* and is the son of Lloyd and the brother of Beau?

5 December
Rock'n'roll innovator Richard Penniman was born in 1935. By what name is he better known?

6 December
Today in 1917, Finland proclaimed its independence from Russia. What is Finland's capital city?

7 December
Who became Prime Minister of England today in 1783 at the age of 24?

8 December
In which city was John Lennon shot today in 1980?

ON THE BOX

9 December

Ⓐ Today in 1960, the first episode of *Coronation Street* was broadcast. Which fictional Manchester suburb provides the setting for the long-running soap?

Ⓑ Eric Idle *(right)* was starring in the show *Rutland Weekend Television* today in 1976. Two other former Python members, Terry Jones and Michael Palin, also had their own television series. What was it called?

Ⓒ Dame Judi Dench was born today in 1934. What is the name of her actor husband?

● ●

10 December

Dorothy Lamour was born today in 1914. Name two of the *Road* movies which she made in the 1940s and 50s with Bob Hope and Bing Crosby *(left)* ?

135

11 December

Italian film director Carlo Ponti was born today in 1913. What is the name of his actress wife?

12 December

Born today in 1915, which American singer and actor had hits in the 1950s with 'Love And Marriage' and 'Three Coins In A Fountain'?

13 December

Dr Samuel Johnson died today in 1784. Name the work of reference which took him nine years to write.

FAMOUS FACES

14 December

Ⓐ Today in 1981, Sebastian Coe was voted Sportsman of the Year. Earlier in the same year he had broken the world record over which distance?

Ⓑ American tennis player Stan Smith was born today in 1946. In which year did he beat Illie Nastase in the men's singles final at Wimbledon?

© Thora Hird gave birth to this former child star today in 1938. Who is she?

©

D

© This Conservative politician was Prime Minister during the abdication of Edward VIII, and died today in 1947. Name him.

• •

15 December
American actor Don Johnson was born today in 1950. In which stylish TV series did he play Detective James 'Sonny' Crockett?

16 December
American actor Lee van Cleef died today in 1989. In which Spaghetti Western did he star with Clint Eastwood and Eli Wallach?

PICTURE WALL

17 December

Ⓐ Lord Kelvin, inventor of the Kelvin scale, died today in 1907. Of which Scottish University did he become a professor at the age of 22?

Ⓑ Which Dickens novel, published today in 1843, features Marley's ghost?

© English chemist and inventor Sir Humphry Davy was born today in 1778. He was the first person to isolate the metal which has the chemical symbol K. What is it?

Ⓓ Today in 1989, Brazil elected a new President in its first free elections for 29 years. Who is he?

18 December
What is the name given to the archaelogical discovery made in Sussex today in 1912?

19 December
Television personality Eamon Andrews was born today in 1922. On which BBC panel game did he start his career in television?

20 December
Novelist James Hilton died today in 1954. What is the title of his most famous book about a schoolmaster?

21 December
Jane Fonda *(right)* was born today in 1937. She won an Academy Award for her performance as Sally Hyde in which film?

BEAT THE CLOCK

22 December
Beethoven's Fifth and Sixth Symphonies were premièred in Leipzig today in 1808. Who played Beethoven in *Immortal Beloved,* the film about his life?

23 December
Today in 1972, Little Jimmy Osmond, shown in the photograph *(left)* with his family, took 'Long-Haired Lover From Liverpool' to the top of the UK charts. What was his brother Donny's first British number one?

24 December
Today in 1871 the first ever performance of *Aida* was presented in Cairo.
Who wrote it?

25 December
Born today in 1907, Andrew Cruickshank played which character in the TV drama series *Dr Finlay's Casebook*?

26 December
Born today in 1891, name the controversial American novelist whose books include *Tropic of Cancer* and *Tropic of Capricorn*?

27 December
Name the German actress, born today in 1904, who starred with David Bowie in the film *Just a Gigolo*?

28 December
Name King William III's queen, who died today in 1694.

29 December
Born today in 1893, which author and feminist wrote *Testament of Youth*?

30 December
English film director and stage actor Sir Carol Reed was born today in 1906. Who played Bill Sykes in his 1968 Oscar-winning film *Oliver!*?

31 December
Sir Anthony Hopkins *(right)* was born today in 1937. What is the name of the character he played in *The Silence of the Lambs*?

DECEMBER ANSWERS

QUICK FIRE QUESTIONS

1 December
Annie Hall.

2 December
Hello, Dolly!

3 December
Joseph Conrad.

4 December
Jeff Bridges.

5 December
Little Richard.

6 December
Helsinki.

7 December
William Pitt, the Younger.

8 December
New York.

ON THE BOX

9 December
Ⓐ Weatherfield.
Ⓑ *Ripping Yarns.*
Ⓒ Michael Williams.

•••••••••••••••••••••••••

10 December
Road to Singapore, Road to Zanzibar, Road to Morocco, Road to Utopia, Road to Rio, Road to Bali.

11 December
Sophia Loren.

12 December
Frank Sinatra.

13 December
Dictionary of the English Language.

FAMOUS FACES

14 December
Ⓐ 800 metres.
Ⓑ 1972.
Ⓒ Janette Scott.
Ⓓ Stanley Baldwin.

15 December
Miami Vice.

16 December
The Good, the Bad and the Ugly.

PICTURE WALL

17 December
Ⓐ Scottish.
Ⓑ *A Christmas Carol.*
Ⓒ Potassium.
Ⓓ Fernando Collor di Melo.

••••••••••••••••••••••

18 December
The Piltdown Man, which turned out to be a hoax.

19 December
What's My Line

20 December
Goodbye, Mr Chips.

21 December
Coming Home.

BEAT THE CLOCK

22 December
Gary Oldman

23 December
'Puppy Love.'

24 December
Guiseppe Verdi.

25 December
Dr Cameron.

26 December
Henry Miller.

27 December
Marlene Dietrich.

28 December
Queen Mary II.

29 December
Vera Brittain.

30 December
Oliver Reed.

31 December
Hannibal Lecter.